MIAMI MICE

BY JOVIAL BOB STINE
PICTURES BY ERIC GURNEY

ISBN 0-590-40373-7

Text copyright © 1986 by R.L. Stine
Illustrations copyright © 1986 by Eric Gurney
MIAMI MICE is a trademark of Scholastic Inc.
Art direction/design by Diana Hrisinko.
All rights reserved. Published by Scholastic Inc.

12 11 10 9 8 7 6 5 4 3 2 1   11   6 7 8 9/8 0 1/9

Printed in the U.S.A.   24

SCHOLASTIC INC.
New York Toronto London Auckland Sydney

In Miami, Florida, where the sun always shines, the police station was in an uproar. Police Chief Zippy hopped up and down on his desk. "Get me my best policemen!" he yelled. "Call the Miami Mice!"

Call us once,
Call us twice,
Call us both
Miami Mice!

"They're my best policemen," Chief Zippy said. "*And*
they can tap dance!"

"Hey, Ted," Miami Fred asked Miami Ted. "Have you ever seen a banana split?"

"No, Fred," said Miami Ted. "But I've seen an ice cream pop!"

Police Chief Zippy frowned and shook his head.

"They're my best policemen," he said. "And they can tap dance. But they tell TERRIBLE jokes!"

"Which one of you is Fred and which one of you is Ted?" asked the chief.

"It's easy to tell us apart," said Ted. "Fred always wears sunglasses and funny-looking shirts. And *I'm* the one who always stands next to Fred!"

Then Chief Zippy became serious.
"Boys, I'm glad you're here,"
he said. "Someone is trying to
make a MONKEY out of me!
    "Do you know what day this is?"
asked the chief.

    "Yes," said Ted. "It's today."
    "No, Ted," said Fred. "It can't
be today. That was yesterday."
    "Then…" said Ted, "it must be
tomorrow."

Police Chief Zippy pulled out a big wall calendar.
The day was circled in red.

"Today is the Fourth of July," he told them. "It's the day
of the big Fourth of July parade."

"Hooray!" said Ted.

"Hooray!" said Fred.

"Everyone in town will be at the parade," said Chief Zippy. "The Mayor will be there. The Fire Chief will be there. *I* will be there! But we have one little problem....

"THE PARADE HAS BEEN STOLEN!!"

"What?"

"What?"

Police Chief Zippy showed them a big picture of a parade. "This is what the parade should look like," he said.

"Hooray!" said Ted.

"Hooray!" said Fred.

"But our parade is missing," Chief Zippy said. "We can't find it anywhere."

"We can't have the Fourth of July without a parade!" said Ted.

"And we can't have a parade without a parade!" said Fred.

"Boys, I want you to go out there and find our missing parade!" ordered Chief Zippy.

We're not scared,
We're not afraid.
We won't come back
Till we find the parade!

The Miami Mice hurried to their car, a bright red
Mouserati convertible.

"Hey, Fred," asked Ted. "Have you ever seen a hot dog
stand?"

"No, Ted," said Fred. "But I've seen a square dance!"

Police Chief Zippy poked his head out of the station window. "No more terrible jokes — until you bring back our missing parade!" he said.

Fred and Ted sped off
in search of the parade.

"We need a plan,"
said Ted.

ONE WAY

"I've got it," said Fred. "You sneak up from behind and
surround them. Then I'll sneak up from in front and take
them by surprise."
   "No, no," said Ted. "Why don't you sneak up from the
side and surprise them from behind. Then I'll surround
them from in front and sneak up from the side."

"That's no good," said Fred. "Why don't I sneak up from the front and the back. Then you sneak up from the back and the front. Then we'll both surround them and take them by surprise."

"That will never work," said Ted. "I think you should sneak up on all sides. Then I'll surround them and take *you* by surprise."

By this time, they were hopelessly lost....

"We're lost. We'd better look for the ocean. That will help us find our way."

"Ocean?! How will we ever find the ocean??!"

"We'll just keep going," said Ted. "We'll stop everyone
we meet and ask them if they've seen the parade. Then
we'll bring them to the police station and ask them again."
The car was stuck in the sand. So they started to walk.

Soon they came upon two alligators roller-skating in the road.

"Have you seen a parade go by here?" asked Ted.

"No, we haven't," said the alligators.

"Why are you on roller skates?" asked Ted.

"Because we don't have enough money to take the bus," said the alligators.

"You'd better come along with us," said Ted.

Fred and Ted led the alligators down the road. Soon they came upon three pink flamingos.

"Have you seen a parade go by?" Fred asked.

"No," said the flamingos.

"What are you doing here on the beach?" Fred asked.

"Nothing," the flamingos said. "We aren't doing anything."

"Then why are you blushing?" asked Fred. "You'd better come along with us."

Fred and Ted walked along the beach with two alligators on roller skates and three pink flamingos. Soon
they came to three bright green parrots, playing guitars in
a tree.

"Good morning," said Ted.

"Good morning, good morning, good morning," said
the parrots.

We'll walk, we'll search,
We'll dig, we'll climb.
We'll even stay out
Past bedtime!

"What are you doing up there?" asked Fred.
"What are you doing up there?" repeated the parrots.
"Why do you repeat everything we say?" asked Ted.
"Why do you repeat everything we say?" asked the
parrots.
"You'd better come along with us," said Fred.
"You'd better come along with us," said the parrots.

Fred and Ted walked on down the road. They were
followed by three bright green parrots playing guitars,
three pink flamingos, and two alligators on roller skates.
Soon they came to four turtles wearing running shoes.

"Have you seen a parade go by here?" asked Fred.

"No…we…haven't…" the turtles said slowly.

"Why are you in those running shoes?" asked Ted.

"We're…running…away…from…home…"
said the turtles.

"But your homes are on your backs!" said Fred.

"No…wonder…it's…
taking…us…so…long!"
said the turtles.

"You'd better come
along with us," said Fred.

They all walked down the road. The Miami Mice were
followed by four turtles in running shoes, three bright
green parrots playing guitars, three pink flamingos, and
two alligators on roller skates. Soon they came to four
barking greyhounds, going round and round in circles.

"Have you seen a parade go by?" asked Ted.

"No. We can't see anything. We're too dizzy," said the
greyhounds.

"Why are you going round and round in circles?"
asked Ted.

"We're chasing our own tails," said the greyhounds.

"Why are you chasing your own tails?" asked Ted.

"Some day we may catch them," replied the
greyhounds.

"You'd better come along with us," said Fred.

They kept walking. Miami Fred and Miami Ted led the
way, followed by four greyhounds going round and round,
four turtles in running shoes, three bright green parrots
playing guitars, three pink flamingos, and two alligators
on roller skates. Soon they came to six penguins standing
near a pond.

"Have you seen a parade go by?" asked Ted.

"No," said the penguins.

"What are you doing here?" asked Fred.

"We're going for a swim," said the penguins.

"Going for a swim? Then why are you all dressed up?"
cried Fred. "You'd better come along with us!"

They all walked down the road.

"You'd better come with us," Fred said to six squirrels
playing trombones.

"You'd better come with us," Ted said to six geese
on stilts.

"You'd better come with us," they said to five dancing dolphins and five cows in clown costumes.

Fred and Ted led them all into town. They marched
down the busy street. The parrots squawked and
strummed their guitars. The cows mooed.

The greyhounds barked. The geese honked. And the
squirrels blew their trombones.
    Everyone came out to watch them march by. The
crowd cheered and clapped.

When Fred and Ted reached the police station, Chief Zippy ran up to them.

"Congratulations!" he said. "That was the best Fourth of July parade this town has ever had!"

"Gee, thanks, chief," the Miami Mice replied.

"But there is just one little problem..." Chief Zippy said.

Fred and Ted followed the Chief inside.

"I made a small mistake when I read the calendar before," Chief Zippy said. "Today is only the *third* of July!!"

"Only the *third* of July?" cried Fred and Ted.

"Yes," said the Chief. "*Tomorrow* is the day of the big parade. That's why I couldn't find it anywhere."

Fred and Ted looked sad. "We were a day early," they said.

"Hey — don't feel bad, boys," said
Chief Zippy. "That was the best *third* of July
parade this town has ever seen!
I'm really glad I called you."

Call us once,
Call us twice.
Call us both
Miami Mice!

"Hey, Fred," said Ted. "Have you ever seen a
cracker box?"
"No," said Fred. "But I've seen a fruit punch!"
"They're my best policemen," said Chief Zippy.
"And they can tap dance. But they *still* tell
TERRIBLE jokes!!"